Fast and Forever

by David Neufeld

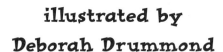

illustrated by
Deborah Drummond

MODERN CURRICULUM PRESS
Pearson Learning Group

Nothing beats light in a race across the universe. Nothing we know of travels faster than light. Nothing! In one second, light can circle the Earth seven times. That's fast!

Perhaps the only thing that can amaze us more than the speed of light is the size of the universe. The size of the universe beats everything—even our ability to imagine it. It goes on forever!

What do you get if you cross the fastest thing around with really long spans of time? You get a light-year. A light-year marks how far light travels in one year. By the way, that distance is six trillion miles. That is *six*, followed by *twelve zeros*. That's 6,000,000,000,000 miles.

Big Dipper

Here on Earth, we get deliveries from the past every night. Let's say all the stars died right now. We can predict what we'd see. The light from the stars we know as the Big Dipper would begin to disappear from the sky when you are quite old. That's because its closest star is about 61 light-years away. A few other stars would wink out before then. But most of the stars in the sky would seem to shine long after your great-great-grandchildren finished fifth grade.

The Big Dipper will make one of its regular deliveries of light to us tonight. That light left its stars anywhere from 61 years ago to over 225 years ago for its star that is farthest from the Earth.

The light you see from the North Star, Polaris (poh-LAIR-us), has been traveling through space even longer. It left before the Pilgrims sailed to Plymouth on the *Mayflower*.

The brightest stars in the sky give us signposts we can identify night after night. People have always imagined pictures in the stars. The stars have inspired fantastic stories of people and animals. Kings, queens, and unfortunate heroes all have their pictures traced in the sky.

There are many star groups in our northern hemisphere. Three would be hard to mistake. This is the way the stars look in the winter.

The Big Dipper points us to the North Star, Polaris. You can see it in all seasons.

The Pleiades (PLEE-uh-deez) is a cluster of related stars, also called the Seven Sisters.

Orion (oh-RYE-un) is known as the hunter. A set of three bright stars forms the hunter's belt. Orion also has a famous nebula (NEB-yoo-lah) inside it. A nebula is a cloud of star dust.

Winter Sky

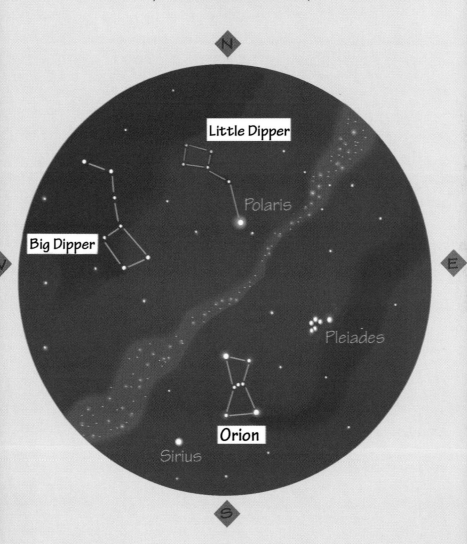

Little Dipper

Polaris

Big Dipper

Pleiades

Orion

Sirius

Big Dipper

You don't need a telescope. You can spot red supergiants, blue giants, double stars, star clusters, nebulas, and galaxies with your eyes alone.

But it is even more fun to look up at space using binoculars. If you look at the second star in the handle of the Big Dipper, you will see it is actually a double star.

The Pleiades is a star cluster with about four hundred stars in it. You can see six of these with your eyes alone. You might see thirty or more with binoculars. The stars in the Pleiades are new stars. They weren't there when the dinosaurs lived.

Pleiades

Orion is well named as "the hunter." Directions to many other stars are given from Orion. Here's one. Go to Orion, find the belt and look downward to the left. The first very bright star in the sky is Sirius (SEER-ee-us).

The light leaving Sirius today won't reach you until you are out of high school.

Looking for a red supergiant? Go straight up from Orion's belt to the top left star. That's Betelgeuse (BEET-el-joos). At the opposite end of Orion, at the bottom right, is Rigel (RYE-jel).

Winter Sky

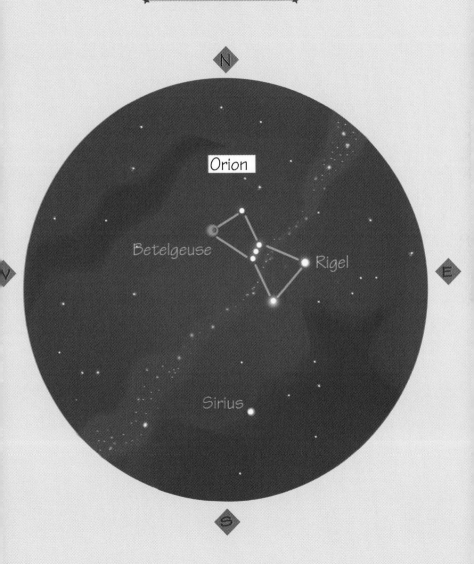

Procyon

Add a Greek word to your vocabulary, Procyon (PRO-see-on). It means "before the dog." This star is only eleven light-years away. The light that arrives today from Procyon has been traveling since about the time you were born.

To find Procyon, go left from Betelgeuse to the first bright star.

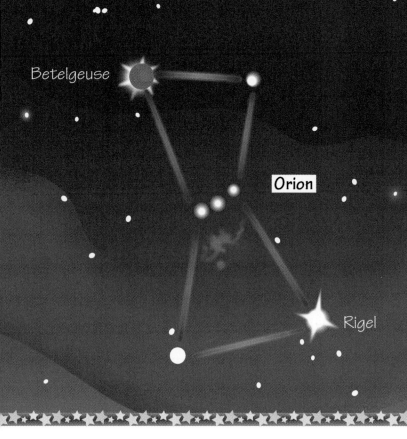

Betelgeuse

Orion

Rigel

Orion contains a great nebula that you can see with binoculars.

It surrounds four visible stars below the belt. It's the Orion Nebula. It was born just fifty thousand years ago. This cloud of gas and dust is still making new stars. You need the darkest of nights to see the nebula clearly.

Orion's belt may be the easiest set of stars to identify. The light we see from them left these stars over nine hundred years ago. Winter is the best time to see Orion's belt.

A sharp-eyed astronomer recently noticed that the three Great Pyramids in Egypt are arranged in a pattern just like the stars in Orion's belt. The size of each Pyramid even matches the brightness of each star.

Other evidence shows that structures inside the Pyramids are aimed right at important stars, like Sirius. The Pyramids may be the oldest star observatories.

Position of pyramids from the air

People have mapped the night sky for a very long time.

Think of a camping trip that lasts forever. After every sunset you have a whole night to look at the sky. You watch as stars change places. Some stars disappear, others appear. They are farther away than we can fathom.

And even tonight, new starlight will arrive from countless light-years away to remind us of forever.